To Olivia:

You are beautiful just the
way you are.

Skin Like Me

By Kay Johnson-Clennon

Skin Like Me is based on a true story.

Livi is curious why no one else in her class has skin like hers.

Skin Like Me

Hello! I am Livi.

Meet my friends – Kolton,
Parker, Ethan and Aubree.

We love the playground.

The playground is where we talk
about serious matters.

Yesterday we talked about our pets.

Today, we talked about why
no one else has skin like me.

I told my parents what we
spoke about today.

My Mummy and Daddy
said that it is ok to have
different skin colours.

I asked my parents if I have
blue eyes like Kolton.

My Mummy and Daddy said
I have brown eyes and we
are all beautiful.

A few weeks later...

Our teacher introduced Anylah to
the class.

On the playground that day, Anylah told us that a storm destroyed her home and she is staying with relatives.

I told my parents about Anylah and that
we had so much fun today.

Anylah and I played and talked all day!

My parents asked who is Anylah.

Anylah is my new friend at school. She has the same skin as me!

I was happy to know that I was not the only kid in the world that has skin like mine.

The End

About the Author: Kay is also a Wife, Mother, Educator and Associate Actuary. She is a Jamaican girl whose calling and purpose in life are to encourage and support people.

Obsessed with variety and learning is one way she describes herself. Blogging, volunteering, and teaching are only but a few of her interests.

www.ingramcontent.com/pod-product-compliance
Lightning Source LLC
Chambersburg PA
CBHW042130110726
48006CB00003B/829